SANTIAGO THE DREAMER

in

LAND AMONG THE STARS

BY RICKY MARTIN

ILLUSTRATED BY PATRICIA CASTELAO

Celebra Children's Books • an imprint of Penguin Group (USA) LLC

CELEBRA CHILDREN'S BOOKS
Published by the Penguin Group
Penguin Group (USA) LLC
345 Hudson Street, New York, New York 10014

USA / Canada / UK / Ireland / Australia / New Zealand / India / South Africa / China

penguin.com
A Penguin Random House Company

ISBN 978-0-451-41571-4

Manufactured in the USA

1 3 5 7 9 10 8 6 4 2

Designed by Jasmin Rubero
Text set in Hadriano Std

For every child . . . may you always follow your dreams
and land among the stars!

Santiago's biggest dream, for as long
as he could remember, was to be on stage.

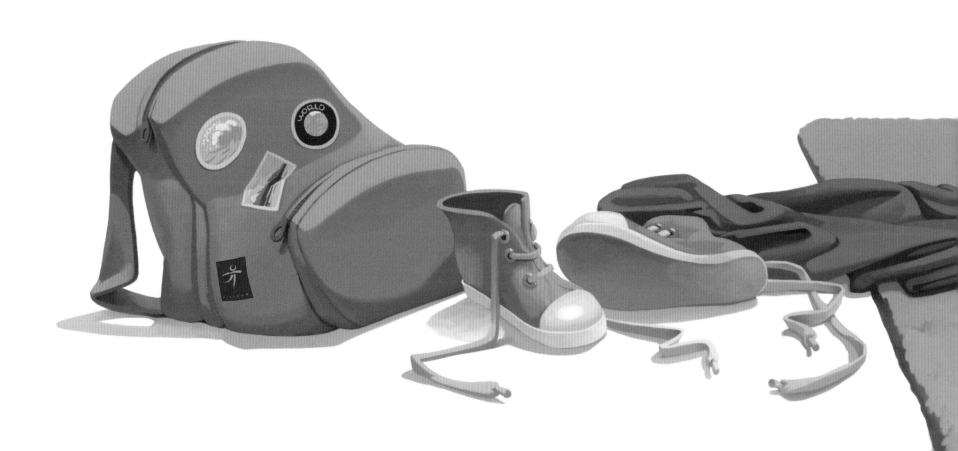

One day at school, auditions were announced for the lead part in the annual play.

Santiago rushed to the auditorium and saw another boy performing, who was just amazing.

The director called Santiago next. But he was so nervous he could barely get out a sound. And when he did, his voice cracked. The kids laughed in response.

The director silenced the students, and Santiago was dismissed.

That night, Santiago broke the news to his father: "I didn't get the part."

Santiago's father gave him a smile and said: "Never give up. You can do anything you dream of, as long as you do it with love. And, no matter what you choose, always reach for the moon!"

Santiago closed his eyes, fell asleep, and started to dream . . .

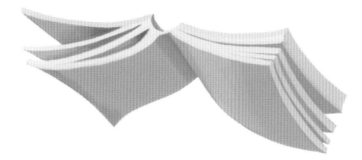

He was in a classroom, but only this time
he was the teacher—helping kids to follow their own dreams.
Teaching them math and science and art . . .

Suddenly, the dream changed, and now
he was in a cockpit flying a big jet . . .

Then he was a doctor helping everyone feel better . . .

Next, he was floating in outer space as an
astronaut making new discoveries . . . .

Soon he was studying dinosaur fossils as a paleontologist . . .

Crack! He just hit a grand slam to win the World Series! Hooray, Santiago!

But the last dream was the one he loved the most:
He was performing on stage at a famous theater.

Santiago was excited about his dream and decided to practice as if he got the lead . . .

Singing while walking home from school . . .

Dancing while doing his chores . . .

Acting in his bedroom.

On the morning of the play, the lead actor lost his voice and couldn't perform.

Santiago quickly found the director and said, "I can do it!"

"Are you sure? Do you know all the lines?" asked the director.

Without hesitating, Santiago said, "I'm ready."

Santiago put all of his heart and soul
into his performance.

At the end of the show, the crowd rose
to their feet and cheered as Santiago took
a bow:

Bravo! Excellent! Magnificent!

After the show, Santiago's father rushed backstage.
"Santiago! How did you learn all the lines and do everything so well?"

"Dad," Santiago said, "you taught me to never give up, to follow my dreams, and to always reach for the moon. And tonight I learned another important lesson."

"What is it?" asked his father.

"That sometimes, when you reach for the moon,
you can land among the stars."